D0448006

Seldovia
Sam

and the

Wildfire Escape

WRITTEN BY
Susan Woodward Springer • ILLUSTRATED BY
Amy Meissner

Alaska Northwest Books®
Portland • Anchorage

To Marie Elyse Hoopes. Read, Dream, Live!
— S. W. S.

For Brian—who never questioned why his muddy bike was
parked on the rug in my studio.
— A. C. M.

Text © 2005 by Susan Woodward Springer
Illustrations © 2005 by Amy Meissner

Library of Congress Cataloging-in-Publication Data

Springer, Susan Woodward.
    Seldovia Sam and the wildfire escape / by Susan Woodward Springer ;
illustrated by Amy Meissner.
        p. cm. — (The misadventures of Seldovia Sam ; 3)
Summary: Sam rides to the rescue of a neighbor's kittens when a careless
camper starts a wildfire that threatens the town of Seldovia itself.
    ISBN 0-88240-601-9 (softbound)
    [1. Wildfires—Fiction. 2. Seldovia (Alaska)—Fiction. 3. Alaska—Fiction.]
I. Meissner, Amy, ill. II. Title III. Series: Springer, Susan Woodward.
Misadventures of Seldovia Sam ; 3.
    PZ7.S768465Sg 2005
    [Fic]—dc21   2004024239

Alaska Northwest Books®
An imprint of Graphic Arts Center Publishing Company
P.O. Box 10306, Portland, Oregon 97296-0306
503-226-2402 • www.gacpc.com

President: Charles M. Hopkins
General Manager: Douglas A. Pfeiffer
Associate Publisher: Sara Juday
Editorial Staff: Timothy W. Frew, Tricia Brown, Kathy Howard,
    Jean Bond-Slaughter
Production Staff: Richard L. Owsiany, Susan Dupere

Editor: Michelle McCann
Cover design: Andrea L. Boven / Boven Design Studio, Inc.; Elizabeth Watson
Interior design: Andrea L. Boven / Boven Design Studio, Inc.; Jean Andrews

Printed in the United States of America

Contents

Bering
Sea

Arctic Circle

Yukon River

Kuskokwim River

Susitna River

Mount △
McKinley

Anchorage

Homer

SELDOVIA

Kodiak

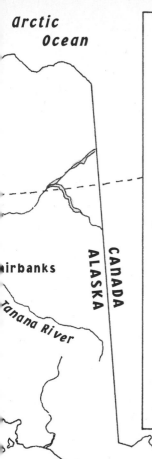

Arctic
Ocean

irbanks

Tanana River

CANADA

ALASKA

Alaska is so big that if you could lay it on top of the
continental United States, it would cover one-fifth
of all of the other states. And there really is a place
called Seldovia. It's about 250 miles south of
Anchorage. But there are no roads to get there.
To reach Seldovia you have to fly in a plane or take
a boat. Some of the place-names in Sam's stories
are real; others are made up. Like Sam's parents,
lots of men and women in Seldovia fly Bush planes
and fish commercially. Is there a real Sam Peterson
in Seldovia? Not by that name. But there's a
little bit of Sam in all the kids in Seldovia, just as
I suspect there's a little bit of Sam in you.

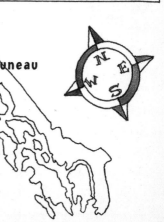

★ Juneau

Gulf of Alaska

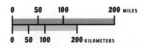

0   50   100   200 MILES

0   50 100   200 KILOMETERS

1

Dry as Dog Biscuits

The May sun sparkling off Kachemak Bay was so bright that Sam had to squint. He was in Homer, helping out at the air service terminal where Mom worked. He did this every summer after school was out, but this year he was getting paid. *I can't wait until I earn enough to buy my X-Treme Trail Smasher!* Sam thought as he sorted a jumble of nuts, bolts, and screws into the jars that the mechanic, Stinky Swenson, had set out for him. Sam was picturing himself racing uphill on his cool new bike, with its knobby tires, fifteen gears, and front suspension.

"How's it going, Sam?" asked Stinky. "Almost done?"

Stinky's voice startled Sam out of his daydream. Sam's dog, Neptune, lifted her head, thinking it might be time to go home.

Stinky chuckled, "What you've done looks good, Sam, but you haven't done much! Think you can finish up before your mom gets back? She's due in soon."

"No problem," Sam said, sitting up straighter and nodding his head. *If I want that bike, it's more work and less daydreaming.*

Sam had just finished when he heard Mom's plane taxi up to the hangar. Neptune recognized it, too, and jumped up, tail wagging.

"Hi Mom!" Sam called as she dropped down from the pilot's seat. She came over for a hug, then spied Sam's greasy hands and grinned. "Better go wash up before you get in the plane. Are you about ready?"

"Yep, I just finished!"

Minutes later, a cleaner Sam was buckling himself into his seat in the blue-and-white Cessna. Neptune was in back. Mom checked her gauges, then taxied to the runway and pushed the power throttle forward. Gaining speed, she pulled back on the yoke.

Sam watched the ground fall away as they climbed. The radio in the small plane crackled. Through his headphones, Sam could hear Charlie Dreyer growling over the airwaves. Charlie owned the air service where Mom worked.

"November 4486, this is November 171 Delta."

Charlie was calling for Mom. Each plane had a unique number, and Mom's was N4486. Because an "N" could sound like an "M" on the radio, pilots used words instead of the alphabet letters. The word for "N" was "November." Charlie's plane was N171D, so for "D," they said "Delta."

"November 171 Delta," said Mom, "This is November 4486. Go ahead."

"Yeah, I'm inbound to Homer from Windy Bay," Charlie said. "You wouldn't believe how dry these creeks are. Dry as dog biscuits." Sam smiled. Charlie had a colorful way of talking.

"Roger that," Mom replied. "We're headed home to Seldovia and it's dry here, too. That big waterfall at the head of Jakolof Bay is just a trickle."

"Let's hope no one gets careless with a match!" answered Charlie. "What's the weather report?"

Mom told him the latest weather fax at Homer showed no rain anytime soon.

Sam knew this was unusual for May. In past years, as they flew over the mountains, he and his mom would see who could spot the most waterfalls created by the melting snow. But now as he looked down, the mountains were nearly bare. Below him, Sam spied Jakolof Bay and the long dirt road that linked Seldovia with the bay's boat dock. It was a favorite spot for boaters. He saw boats, clam diggers, tents, and campfires.

Sam thought hard about those fires at the edge of the dry woods. Dad had taught him the special formula for putting out a campfire: first the bucket of seawater, then the sand kicked onto the fire to bury it, and last, another bucket of seawater poured carefully over the top. Dad would repeat his formula: *"No air + no fuel = no fire!"*

It was important to put out campfires the right way. He hoped the city people camping at Jakolof Bay knew Dad's special formula.

2

A Wisp of Smoke

The next morning, Sam's dad and his crew were preparing to go herring fishing. Dad was packing canned goods and bags of pasta while his helpers carried armloads of fishing gear to the truck. Tomorrow they would leave for a month on the *Wild Rose,* headed for the fishing grounds near Kodiak Island.

Mom was paying bills, while Sam munched on cereal. The kitchen radio was tuned to the Homer station. After a moment of silence, the announcer's voice changed.

"We've just received word of a major

wildfire west of Anchorage. Here's what we know so far . . ."

Sam called, "Mom, Dad! Come 'ere! There's a big fire!"

Both of his parents stopped to listen.

". . . fifty miles west of Anchorage is burning out of control due to continuing dry conditions. Firefighters and equipment from Anchorage and the Kenai Peninsula are helping combat the blaze. More later as details . . ."

Dad shook his head. "Bad news. I sure hope we don't have any fires, especially with everybody working on that one."

Mom nodded. "And with most of our Seldovia men headed out fishing, we'd really be in a pickle. What we need is some rain." She sighed, "Well, Sam, we'd better get going."

Sam jumped up. Work meant money to buy the X-Treme Trail Smasher. His old bike was okay, but it didn't have extra gears for climbing hills, or shocks for taking jumps. Dad had repaired his frame or a broken chain more than once.

He had chuckled, "Sam I'd tell you to go easy on this old bike, but I know better. Just to try to slow down a little bit, okay?"

Sam had grinned and agreed . . . sort of.

In Homer, Sam washed windows. Everything got dirty quickly from all the dust and sand blowing around. *A little rain would sure help me, too,* he thought.

At day's end, Sam and Neptune piled into Mom's plane. He fastened his seat belt, put on his headphones, and gave Mom the "thumbs-up" sign. Aloft, the little plane bounced in the bumpy air. Sam loved it. It was kind of like jumping his bike.

"Woo-hoo!" he yelled happily.

Mom pulled her headphones away and looked a little cross. "Please don't yell in my ear, Sam. It's been a long day."

Flying over Jakolof Bay, Sam noticed that the busy beach was now deserted. Then he spotted a wisp of smoke at the edge of the trees. Without thinking, he yelled into his headset.

"Mom! Look! I see smoke!"

This time, she didn't fuss about him yelling in her ear.

"Hang on. I'm going to get a better look."

Sam felt his stomach rise as Mom forced the plane to dive. She turned the yoke hard to the right and circled above the smoke in a tight turn.

"It's a fire, all right," she said. "I can't see any campers though. I'd better call it in, just to be safe. Homer base, this is November 4486."

"November 4486, this is Homer base, go ahead," Charlie answered.

"We're seeing some smoke at Jakolof Bay, just up from the dock. I've circled it and don't see any people. Can you get it checked out?"

"Roger, will do," confirmed Charlie, "I'm on it."

Mom flew over the last ridge and landed on Seldovia's airstrip. They climbed in the Jeep and headed home.

"Hi Squirt!" Dad said at the door. He squeezed Sam's shoulder, then turned to Mom. "Charlie called. A trooper checked

out your smoke. He found the campers nearby, and he warned them to watch it."

Dad dished up venison stew, then he and Mom spent the evening mending herring nets in the living room while Sam read a stunt bike magazine. That night he dreamed of jumping the X-Treme Trail Smasher through big rings of smoke.

3

A Fire Is Reborn

It was still dark when Dad sat on Sam's bed. Sam yawned and rubbed one eye.

"Why are you leaving so early? I thought we were all going down to the dock together."

"The wind came up on the bay. I want to cross open water and get behind Kodiak Island before it gets worse. I'll be fine. Just give me a hug."

After Dad left, Sam instantly fell asleep again. Several hours later, he woke to the sound of tree branches thumping against the house. Bright sunlight flooded the room. *Another windy, dry day. Dry as dog biscuits.* Sam quickly dressed and Neptune followed him to the kitchen, where Mom sipped coffee.

"'Morning, Sam! I thought I was going to have to wake you up for our date."

On Mom's day off, they always had breakfast at The Tidepool, which looked out over the harbor and was decorated with shells and crabs and pieces of coral. Today the restaurant was crowded and everyone was talking about the weather and herring fishing.

Sam was making a racetrack with his fork in what was left of his scrambled eggs, when Billy Sutton trotted in.

"Hey Sam," said Billy. "You ready to go jumping?"

Sam glanced at his mom, who was chatting with Melody Chambers's mom. Sam wasn't crazy about know-it-all Melody, but their moms were good friends, so he saw Melody more often than he liked.

"Boys, did you know Melody's cat, Willow, had kittens?" Mrs. Chambers asked. "They're ready for new homes. How'd you like a kitten?"

Sam already knew the answer. Neptune would never forgive him. He looked outside, where she waited patiently. Neptune wagged her tail as if to say, *No kittens! Just you and me!*

"Umm . . . thanks, we'll think about it," stuttered Sam.

After promising to ride safely and be good and be home for lunch and a whole bunch of other things, the boys made their escape.

"Let's go out to my house," Billy said. "I made some awesome ramps!"

"Cool!" agreed Sam.

With Neptune chasing, the boys rode nearly two miles out the dirt road. Sam watched Billy shift gears and climb hills easily, while he stood on his pedals and pumped his three-speed. *Not long until I have my X-Treme Trail Smasher!* he thought.

They passed dozens of new houses. Out here, the logging company had cut big stands of trees and built new roads, then sold the land. There were still lots of stumps and a few dead trees around, but families like Billy's and Melody's were happy to find land and build modern homes with hard-earned fishing money.

Billy's house looked like a mansion to Sam, with lots of different-shaped windows that reflected the sun. There was no lawn yet—just stumps and parts of trees. Billy had set plywood against some stumps to make his bike stunt course. They took turns sailing off the ramps until Sam was sore from his bike jarring each time he landed. When he borrowed Billy's bike, with its big

shock absorbers, it felt like landing on a mattress. Sam was almost relieved when Billy said, "I'm hungry!"

Sam looked at his watch. It was past noon—he'd promised to be home for lunch.

"Let's go to my house," he said. "I'll race you! At least I have a chance going down the hill!"

When Sam and Billy burst through the kitchen door, they were laughing and hungry as bears. Mom was taking notes with the phone tucked under her ear. She waved her hand at them to be quiet.

"Okay," she said, "I'll get going now." She hung up and turned to the boys. "That was Charlie. Remember that campfire? The campers didn't put it out all the way, and now it's spreading. They want me to fly over and check it."

Sam had never seen his mom look so worried.

4

Worst Fears Confirmed

Mom gathered her pilot's notebook, headphones, and key, then grabbed her jacket.

"Mom, wait!" said Sam, "Billy and I can help spot the fire."

"Oh, Sam," she said, "it's too windy and rough."

Sam knew Mom would take him in an instant. He flew all the time. But would Billy get sick?

"Don't worry about me, Mrs. Peterson," Billy said. "My mom says my stomach is like a steel drum. She's a nurse, so she oughta know. I won't get sick, I promise."

Sam's mom looked hard at Billy, then picked up the phone. "Okay, but let's call your mom first."

Billy spotted the chocolate-frosted brownies on the counter and each boy grabbed a couple. They stuffed one in their mouths and the other in a napkin in their jackets.

Then Mom said, "Let's go!" and two excited boys jumped on their bikes to follow her Jeep to the airstrip.

In the plane, Sam sat in the copilot's seat. He gave Billy a pair of headphones and plugged them in. They pulled their

seat belts tight. Billy's hand slid in his jacket pocket and he crammed the second brownie in his mouth.

Mom taxied to the runway and revved the engine. The engine noise was loud as they roared down the runway and, at the very end, lifted off.

After a bumpy ride, Jakolof Bay came into view, and Sam spotted it right away. The white wisp they'd seen yesterday was now a big chimney of thick gray smoke.

Mom spoke through the headphones. "I'm going to circle the smoke. Watch and tell me if you see flames. Billy, try not to stare at the ground as I'm turning. Just glance down, then look back up at the controls for a minute. Otherwise you may get sick, okay?"

"Okay, Mrs. Peterson." Billy's voice sounded small.

Mom tilted the yoke and held it as

the plane made a tight circle. They bounced in the wind, and it was hard for Sam to keep his eyes on the right spot. Suddenly the wind parted the column of smoke.

"I see fire, Mom!" he exclaimed.

"Me, too," croaked Billy.

"Okay, I'm going to circle a couple more times. If you can, tell me how many trees are burning."

As Mom circled again, the plane bucked and jumped, and there was a gap in the smoke for a moment. Then the wind shifted again and the gap closed.

"Mom, I think there's five trees on fire. I know I saw two trees that were all burned up," reported Sam.

"Uhhhhh ..." added Billy.

Mom straightened the plane and turned toward Seldovia. "Good job, boys. Let's go. It's rough!"

She pushed the transmit button and called Charlie. "Better get word to the sheriff," she said. "It's too big to handle without a crew."

"Roger, roger," replied Charlie. "The sheriff already has a call in to the Homer Ranger Station to get a crew together.

It's hard—everyone's at the fire up north."

"Charlie, we'd better act fast. Too many dead trees and not enough melting snow. If that fire gets bigger and jumps the canyon, it could burn all the way into town."

"And take all those fancy new houses with it," added Charlie, not knowing that Billy was in the plane. Sam turned to look at his friend. There was a look of horror on Billy's face.

Billy moaned, then threw up his two brownies, and his breakfast, and who knows what else all over the backseat.

5

The Battle Begins

On the ground, Sam couldn't wait to open his door. *Phew! The smell in there!* Billy climbed out looking pale and kind of shaky.

"Sorry. I've never done that before."

Mom sighed. "That's okay, but maybe next time you should go easy on the brownies."

"Yes'm," mumbled Billy. "I guess I'll go to the clinic and see my mom."

"Good idea," replied Mom, "and Billy ...? Don't worry about your house, okay?"

Billy smiled a wobbly smile and pedaled

away. Mom pulled out the seats while Sam grabbed the hose. Soon they were clean and drying in the warm sun.

Just then, a big, yellow Cessna taxied up. "Why, that's Charlie!" exclaimed Mom.

He cut the engine and two strangers stepped out. Charlie came around to introduce them.

"Rose, this is Mitch with the Homer Ranger Station, and Preston, the chief at the Homer Fire Department. We're headed to a meeting in town—looking for volunteer firefighters. You comin'?"

"Most of our men are out fishing," Mom answered. "Can't you send a crew from Homer while the fire is still small?"

Charlie gently answered, "Rose, it's not small anymore, and it's spreading."

"Is . . . is it headed in this direction?" she asked. All three nodded solemnly.

"Then we'd better get going."

The hall was packed and noisy when they arrived. The mayor cleared his throat, welcomed everyone, and introduced the visitors. Mitch spoke first.

"The winds are pushing the fire this way. I've pulled a crew from the fire up north—but they won't get here 'til the day after tomorrow."

Preston stood. "Five men from the Homer Fire Department are coming in the morning. I just need fifteen volunteers. With my guys as leaders, that will give us five crews of four men each."

Preston looked around. So did Sam. So did everyone else. Most were older men, or city people who owned the summer cabins, and a few shop owners. They didn't look very rugged.

If only Dad and the other fishermen were here! thought Sam.

In the end, five men and three women

stepped forward. That was just half of what was needed!

The sheriff called for attention. He was the size of two men, with a belly like Santa.

"I'm a big fella," he began, and several people chuckled, "but I can run a backhoe and I'm good at it. Give me some people to work the ridge. We'll cut a wide path that the fire can't cross. We'll drop trees with chainsaws, then I'll pull stumps with my machine."

There were murmurs of agreement.

"Creating a fire break is a good idea," said Mitch. "Without trees to burn, the fire goes out. But if we fight the fire at Jakolof Bay, it may not even get to that ridge."

A man stood up, "What do you mean, 'may not'! Can you give us a guarantee?"

Melody's mom called out, "What about our new houses out the road? Aren't they important?"

"What about my summer cabin?" yelled another man.

"Forget the summer cabins," cried another. "We want to protect our town!"

Sam had never seen these neighbors so upset. Then the sheriff spoke again: "Well, you fellows can go throw water

around at Jakolof. I'm taking my backhoe and my crew, and we're going up the ridge to save this town." He marched out with his followers.

It was all mixed up after that. Mrs. Chambers asked again about the new houses, but her voice was lost in the noise. The meeting ended with the mayor calling out instructions for volunteers.

Sam glanced over at Melody. Tears rolled down her cheeks. Even though she was a know-it-all, she didn't look like one right now. She looked scared, and Sam felt sorry for her.

All around him, Sam heard: "What's going to happen?" He wondered, too. His head was so full it made him dizzy to think!

6

Our Best Shot

S am!" called Mom up the stairs. "Sa-a-a-m! Time to get up!"

Sam groaned and blinked. He hadn't slept well, but Mom sounded serious and on the verge of being mad. Sam rolled out of bed and thumped downstairs.

"What's going on?" he asked sleepily.

"Sam, listen carefully," said Mom grimly. Sam realized she had her jacket on and her flying things were on the counter.

"I'm going to be in the air all day. Charlie needs extra help to bring the firefighters and their gear over from Homer. Then I'll

have to fly over the fire and send reports to the ground crews."

"Can I go with you?" asked Sam. He knew the answer would be "No," but he tried anyway.

"No, Sam," replied Mom. "I'm going to need every seat in the plane."

"But I could help you . . ." began Sam, but Mom cut him off.

"No, Sam, you have to stay here. The mayor may decide to evacuate the town if this fire gets close. I want you at the clinic so Billy's mom can keep an eye on you."

"What do you mean, 'evacuate'?" asked Sam. "Where would we go?"

"If that happens, and I mean *if,* they'll get some boats rounded up and you'll head out in the bay."

Sam was wide awake now, and he felt his stomach jump.

"But, Mom, wait," Sam pleaded. "Can't

you just land and pick up Neptune and me?"

Sam's mother knelt and put her hands on his shoulders. "If that fire makes it to the top of the ridge, it'll be too dangerous for me to land." She hugged him and kissed his forehead. "You'll be okay, Sam, and so will I. Don't worry. Just promise me you'll listen to Mrs. Sutton and do exactly as she says. So get dressed—she's coming to pick you up. And be sure to take extra warm clothes and Neptune's leash. I love you."

Sam nodded. He could feel tears filling his eyes. He rubbed them hard with his fists. Mom kissed him again and then she was out the door. Sam noticed she was carrying a shoebox—her memory box, she called it—where she kept her favorite family pictures and art stuff that Sam had made. As he dressed, he decided to put some of his favorite things in his backpack, too: a fossil of a clamshell, Neptune's puppy collar, and his worn-out, one-eyed teddy bear.

Sam waited on the sidewalk. Main Street was full of people bringing stuff to the docks. He recognized many of them as people from new homes out on the road where Billy and Melody lived. There were lots of boxes, and a rocking chair, and a computer, and an old mirror. How would they ever fit everything on the boats? There were hardly enough boats left in the harbor for just the people. He wondered if Billy would get to bring his new bike.

Two strangers passed him, their faces and clothes black with soot. Sam guessed they might be firefighters. They didn't even notice him. ". . . fire's jumped Dark Creek Canyon," said one man. "Already burned six houses out there."

Sam shivered.

7

Where Will It Stop?

The sight of Billy and his mom pulling up in their red pickup was a huge relief. And there was Billy's bike perched on top of a pile of stuff in the back.

Mrs. Sutton rolled down her window. "Hop in, Sam. We're headed for the clinic, and you boys will need to stay there. If we have to go to the harbor, I don't want to go searching for you two."

Sam opened the tailgate for Neptune. He was about to climb into the truck when he remembered his mom's instructions. "Just a minute, Mrs. Sutton," he said.

"I forgot something!"

Sam ran inside and found his jacket and an old fleece vest of Dad's. He pulled Neptune's leash off its nail, then took a quick look around the kitchen. He grabbed a picture of his parents smiling from the deck of the *Wild Rose*. He stuffed it all into his pack with his other treasures and headed out. They were already at the clinic when he realized—he'd forgotten his own bike!

The vacant lot next to the clinic was a gathering place for families from out the road. As the fire burned toward their houses, they had packed and fled into town. Sam noticed some were dabbing at tears and snuffling quietly.

He wandered among people who stood in groups near piles of their belongings. A man with a clipboard was calling out and checking off names when he heard "Here!"

"Chambers!" he called. "Anybody seen them?" Sam looked around. No Mrs. Chambers; no Melody. Actually, he had lost track of Billy and his mom, too. But they were probably in the clinic. The man went on calling other names, but everyone else answered.

Where were Melody and her mom? Sam walked around the crowd again. They had to be here. But he didn't see them. He was looking so hard that he almost tripped over a heap of duffle bags and cardboard boxes. A cat carrier slid to the ground. The upset cat inside meowed loudly.

"Melody's kittens!" Sam murmured. At that moment, Sam made an important decision. First he thought he'd ask Billy's mom to drive out to look for Mrs. Chambers and Melody. Then he saw their red pickup loaded with stuff—and Billy's bike on top.

The bike! Billy's fast, lots-a-gears, big

shocks, hot red bike! There it was, ready to go. Sam looked at the ridge and the smoke drifting toward town. It would take too long to go home for his own bike, then slowly pedal all the way to Melody's. Without a second thought, Sam pulled Billy's bike down and set out as fast as his legs would move. Neptune ran at his side, her tongue flapping and dripping.

Sam shifted the gears so he could climb the hilly road faster. Even so, by the time he reached the Chambers's house, he was standing on the pedals and his chest was heaving. The air was smoky, and trees burned on each side of the road.

Mrs. Chambers's station wagon was loaded with bags and boxes, but Sam couldn't see anybody. Then Melody and her mom appeared out of the smoke, hands cupped to their mouths, calling "Willow! W-i-i-l-l-o-o-w!"

They spotted Sam. "Oh Sam!" cried Melody, "We can't find Willow and her kittens!"

Just then, a noise like a gunshot startled them all. They turned to see a burning tree snap and fall, almost blocking the road.

"Melody, we can't wait any more!" said Mrs. Chambers. "Let's hope Willow found someplace safe to hide her kittens."

"I won't leave her!" Melody sobbed. Sam could see she was almost hysterical. Even though he wasn't crazy about cats and he was even less crazy about Melody, his heart tightened. Right now they needed a miracle, and fast!

8

Dogs, Cats, and a Miracle

Mrs. Chambers put her arm tightly around Melody's shoulders and steered her toward the car. Melody covered her face with her hands and sobbed. Sam looked around—now where was Neptune? *What was it with dogs and cats, disappearing in the blink of an eye?!*

Sam ran around to the backyard, calling for his dog. Just as he was starting to panic, he heard barking. "Neptune! Come on!" Sam yelled.

At the corner of the big back porch, he saw his dog, head shoved under the steps, front paws digging, dirt flying through the smoky air.

"Neptune, come on!" Sam yelled again. "This is no time to be chasing squirrels!"

Squirrels. Kittens. *Oh, my gosh!* thought Sam, *Melody's kittens!*

He raced back around to the driveway. Mrs. Chambers and Melody were waiting for him in the car. "I think Neptune found Melody's kittens," cried Sam. "Under the back porch!"

Without waiting for an answer, he ran back to Neptune. By the slam of two car doors he could tell Mrs. Chambers and Melody were coming behind him.

Sam skidded to a halt. Neptune had disappeared but there was a big pile of dirt by the porch steps. Melody and her Mom almost crashed into Sam. He opened his mouth to explain, but before he could, Neptune crawled out from under the

porch with . . . a tiny mewling kitten in her mouth!

"Oh, Neptune, you're wonderful!" exclaimed Melody. She gently took the kitten from Neptune. It was wet with dog slobber and shivering, but otherwise unharmed.

Neptune dove back under the porch. Sam fell to his stomach and shimmied under,

too. As his eyes adjusted to the dark, he could see Willow and the other six kittens way back against the foundation. One by one, Neptune picked up the kittens, and Sam grabbed them and handed them out to Melody and her mom.

Only when one kitten was left did Willow pick it up herself and crawl out into the gray daylight. Mrs. Chambers swooped Willow and the last kitten into her arms before the cat had a chance to change her mind.

Coughing, eyes stinging, they sprinted for the car as spruce trees ignited with a loud "Whoosh!" Sam, Melody, and Neptune squeezed in among the bags and boxes, with Willow and her kittens.

Gravel flew as Mrs. Chambers put the car in reverse and pealed out of the driveway. Burning trees had fallen nearby but luckily none of them blocked their path. Mrs. Chambers swerved left and right, like she was driving in a video game.

As they neared town, the road widened and no trees burned along its edges.

"Phew!" exclaimed Mrs. Chambers. "That was a close call. Neptune, you are truly a hero, and Willow is a very lucky cat."

Melody wrapped her arms around

Neptune and hugged her. "Neptune, you're the best dog in the whole world. I love you!"

Sam was proud of Neptune, too. This day just might turn out okay, despite the fire. It was a good thing he'd grabbed Billy's fast, fancy bike when he did.

Oh, no. Billy's bike. The fast, fancy, expensive red bike that was still at Melody Chambers's house! Sam groaned and hung his head. *Oh, no. Oh, no. Oh, no . . .*

State Ferry to the Rescue

Melody chattered nonstop. She was too happy and sad and relieved to notice Sam's dismay. When they reached the clinic, Sam threw open his door to escape. He mumbled, "Um, I'll tell them you're here," and hurried toward the clipboard man.

Moments later, he heard his name: "Sam! Sam! Over here!" Billy and Mrs. Sutton were waving wildly. Sam jogged over, feeling sick. He started to speak, but Mrs. Sutton shushed him. "Sam, we've been looking all over! Where have you been?"

"I was . . . I didn't . . . I . . ." Sam tried to explain, but Mrs. Sutton was talking nervously. "The mayor gave the order to evacuate, and the state car ferry heard about the fire, and they changed course to help us, and it just got here, and they're loading everybody up. We'll drive the truck on. Are you okay? Where's your dog?"

"Right here," said Sam.

"Load her in the back and let's go," she said. "Sure you're okay?" Neither one of them had noticed that Billy's bike wasn't in the truck.

The big blue ferry was full of people and cars and animals. Crewmembers ran around and urged drivers to load their vehicles quickly. Normally, boarding the ferry was a great adventure for Sam and his friends. There were so many places to explore. Today, as soon as they could, the boys went up on deck.

"This'll be cool, won't it, Sam?" grinned Billy. Sam looked at his best friend. Billy had just lost his home, but he was still so cheery. He was always in a good mood. Would Billy still be grinning when he learned his beloved bike was, at this very moment, melted into a heap of useless metal?

He groaned at the thought.

"What's wrong, Sam?" asked Billy. "You're not getting seasick, are you? We haven't even left the dock!"

Sam sighed. This wasn't going to be easy. "Billy, I have to tell you something. About your bike. It's . . . it's . . . not in the truck. It's gone."

"My bike? Where is it then?" gulped Billy.

"I used it to go find Melody and her mom. They didn't show up at the clinic, and I had to see if they were okay." In a rush, Sam told his friend about the wild bike ride, and the fire, and the search for

Melody's cat, and Neptune digging under
the porch. He told Billy about the smoke,
pulling the kittens to safety, and the burning trees on the road.

"Melody was screamin' her head off and Mrs. Chambers was yelling to get in the car. I totally forgot about your bike. I'm so sorry. It's all my fault."

"I can't believe it. D-do you think maybe the fire could have burned around it?" Billy asked hopefully.

Sam shook his head. "I don't think so. It was leaning against the house, and I think . . . their house is probably gone now." Sam's voice cracked. The events of the day were catching up with him. He was worn out and scared, and missing his mom and dad.

Billy's voice cracked a little, too. "That's all right, Sam. I guess you had to go help them. You're still my friend, okay?" Billy gave a shaky smile.

Sam smiled back. Just then a crew lady came over and said, "Boys, we've got cookies and hot chocolate in the galley.

Why don't you come inside? It's getting blustery out here."

With her words, a gust hit the ferry. Above them, Sam saw thick, dark clouds. White spray was topping the waves in the bay, and the sun was falling behind the mountains. Looking back toward town, Sam gasped, "Billy, look!"

Billy and the crew lady stopped and turned. Sam pointed to the ridge above town. It was glowing red! Would Seldovia burn next?

Gifts Given
and Received

That night, the winds brought heavy, low clouds that dumped a cold rain. Billy crawled out of his sleeping bag and peeked outside.

"Sam, the fire's out!" He pointed to the ridge top. It was smoking, but the awful red glow was gone. The firebreak that the sheriff had cleared, together with the wind and the rainstorm, had stopped the fire! The ferry was steaming toward town, where Mom was waiting on the docks.

After what seemed like forever, she was hugging Sam tightly. "Oh, Sam, I'm so glad to see you!" she said. Sam wanted to tell her about the fire and the wild bike ride and Melody's kittens and Neptune, the hero, but it would have to wait.

Now Mom turned to hug Mrs. Sutton. "You'll stay with us, of course, until you get resettled. Come on, I'll make some tea."

"We're gonna watch stuff here, okay Mom?" Only one boy asked, but both mothers nodded as they left.

When Sam looked back at the water, he spied one, then four, then more fishing boats chugging into Seldovia Bay. And there was the *Wild Rose!*

"They must have heard about the fire on the radio!" Sam cried. "Let's go!"

"Yeah, let's get our bikes!" said Billy, and then he remembered. His smile faded. So did Sam's. *Could Billy really ever forgive him?*

One by one, the boat captains guided their vessels into their slips. Here came

Dad! Here came Mr. Sutton! Once the boats were tied up, the engines shut down, the gear bags unloaded, and everybody hugged, they started walking home.

"Where's your bike, Billy?" asked Mr. Sutton.

"I, uh . . ." Sam stammered.

Billy interrupted. "It's a long story, Dad. We'll tell you later!" He nudged Sam and the two of them ran ahead to the house.

Sam felt even worse. If only Billy would get mad and yell or something . . . but that wasn't Billy. He would give anything to Sam or anyone else. *What could I give him that would make up for what happened?* thought Sam. Then it came to him: his savings. Sam sighed. It meant good-bye X-Treme Trail Smasher, well, until next summer. *At least I have a bike,* he told himself.

At dinner that night, the mood was light around the crowded table. The picture of

Sam's parents and the *Wild Rose* was back on the wall. The grown-ups were glad that no one had been hurt. The Suttons could rebuild their home.

Billy was finishing the story of Sam and the bike and Neptune's rescue when Sam broke in: "I've been thinking, Billy. I saved all of my job money, and you can have it. It's probably not enough, but . . ."

"Are you sure, Sam?" asked Mr. Sutton.

"I'm sure," Sam replied. Billy was grinning. Dad was nodding and looking really proud. Everyone was nodding and smiling. It felt good, even if his cheeks were getting hot.

Just then there was a knock. It was Melody and Mrs. Chambers. Melody sure had a way of showing up at the wrong time!

But Melody had a surprise. "Sam, I brought you a present. Actually, it's for Neptune, for rescuing Willow's babies." She pulled a gray kitten from her coat.

"I think you should name him 'Little Sparky.'"

Everyone laughed, while Sam rolled his eyes and grumbled, "Well, I think we should call him 'Big Trouble.'" At that instant, the kitten meowed loudly.

Neptune rose from her bed, gently took the kitten in her mouth, and returned to her warm place. The kitten nestled between Neptune's big paws and yawned.

"I think Neptune has a pet," Melody laughed, "and I guess 'Big Trouble' really is his name!"